Metaphorosis

Jan-Mar 2024

Beautifully made speculative fiction

Also from Metaphorosis

Metaphorosis Magazine

Metaphorosis: Best of 20xx
Metaphorosis 20xx: The Complete Stories
annual issues, from 2016
Monthly issues

Plant Based Press

Best Vegan Science Fiction & Fantasy
annual issues, 2016-2020

from B. Morris Allen:
Chambers of the Heart: speculative stories
Susurrus
Allenthology: Volume I
Tocsin: and other stories
Start with Stones: collected stories
Metaphorosis: a collection of stories

Verdage

Reading 5X5 x3: Changes
Reading 5X5 x2: Duets
Score: an SFF symphony
Reading 5X5: Readers' Edition
Reading 5X5: Writers' Edition

Vestige

The Nocturnals, by Mariah Montoya

Joyful Heave

Museum Piece: an unusual collection

Metaphorosis

Jan-Mar 2024

edited by
B. Morris Allen

ISSN: 2573-136X (online)
ISBN: 978-1-64076-278-7 (e-book)
ISBN: 978-1-64076-279-4 (paperback)

Metaphorosis
a magazine of speculative fiction
from
Metaphorosis Publishing

Neskowin

Jan-Mar 2024

... 97, 98, 99, 100!

Metaphorosis has been publishing continuously since 1 January 2016, with a new story every Friday, without fail. The end of 2023, our eighth year, brought us to issue #96. Sometime in 2022, it occurred to me to mark that milestone by doing something special for issues 97-100.

What better to do than to bring back my favorite writers and artists? These are the folks whose work I've been most impressed by, who've been the most fun to work with, and who I think represent what we've tried to achieve with Metaphorosis.

So, in 2024, we'll publish just one story a month (gathered in quarterly print issues), but it'll be a good one! This first issue, #97, gathers writers L. Chan, Evan Marcroft, Vanessa Fog, and artist Candra Hope — all folks I'm proud have a long association with us at Metaphorosis Publishing. I'll have a little more to say about each, but you're in for a treat, both in this issue and the remaining three for the year. Sit back and enjoy!

B. Morris Allen
Editor

A word about L. Chan

We've been lucky enough to to have worked with L. Chan since *Metaphorosis'* very first year. His story "Whalesong" appeared in one of our earliest issues – 15 April 2016, to be precise. It's a seriously sad story about a forlorn and lonely whale and about pollution and responsibility and consequences. I still think about it frequently; it's one of my favorites of the stories we've published.

Happily, that wasn't the end of the relationship. In fact, L. Chan is one of the rare members of the Meta4osis club — authors we've published four or more times.

He next appeared in *Metaphorosis* with "Heartwood" on 05 May 2017, another beautiful story about change and wisdom. In 2018, his story, "The Fourth Pillar Says No" appeared in our anthology, *Reading 5X5*, an unusual and intriguing anthology in which several authors wrote stories from the same prompt, giving insight into how different authors approach the same material.

In 2020, *Metaphorosis* started experimenting with serialized stories, and L. Chan's was the very first we published, with the three part Sonata appearing in January, February, and March of the year, followed quickly by "Seven Scraps Unwritten" in April — an unrelated story, but set in the same universe.

I've enjoyed L. Chan's stories all the way through, and I'm very pleased to be able to present another one now, in these special 2024 issues. Here's the latest, "This is How We Stay Alive".

This is How We Stay Alive

L. Chan

It was the six hundred and thirtieth day after Jeff became a ghost, and things were not going well. Jeff had a routine, as did all the other ghosts. He made coffee, as he liked it, black and without sugar, but the liquid sloshed over the edge of the cup and spilled onto the floor below. Wisps of steam disappeared into the muggy morning air, and lazy sunlight glinted off the crystalline leaves of the plants the Preservation Society had left behind, throwing little rainbows onto the walls of the government flats they crept up.

The mornings were when Pris' absence bit the hardest. Pris had already given Jeff some of the best years of his life, and then after the Preservation Society came and stole one hundredth of the world's population, they'd still had each other. They'd woken up, disembodied and confused, amidst the crystalline alien blossoms that had sprouted in their bed, ghosts in every sense of the word. Finding themselves prisoners, first, of their condition, as they learned to engage the world anew without flesh. Second, of the strange alien garden that now flourished in their bedroom. It anchored them to world, tethering them to their home. They found their ghostly forms fading into incoherence the further they got from their garden. Leaving their home was near unbearable. They fumbled their way through their new existence, while the rest of the world came to terms with the ghosts and discovered how to live with them.

Jeff and Pris had learned. They had adapted, discovered that ghosts could still interact with electrical devices. They had reconnected with the world, finding others like them. Of course, this had been before the Government finally came in with their cleanup crews and their neat little pamphlets in four languages telling ghosts about their new rights (few), their responsibilities (many) and a short catechism on prolonging their newfound existence, helpfully titled 'This is how we stay alive'.

But now Pris was gone, her laptop silent where it had lain for years. Space was scarce in Singapore and there was no room for flats solely occupied by ghosts. Eventually, hastily passed laws allowed the government to seize the flats by eminent domain for reallocation. So Jeff was getting a new roommate.

This is how we stay alive: We acknowledge the Preservation Society has taken our bodies, and we will not get them back.

Hao Ming sat amidst the ruins of someone else's life. He knew what to expect from a haunted apartment, what the ghosts were capable of. Ghosts were nearly impossible to perceive. They had almost no power to manipulate the physical medium, but anything electronic was fair game. And they needed to be near one of those alien plants. In some jurisdictions, panic had set in the first morning after the alien Preservation Society did their work — the populace had set upon the plants with firearms and tools, blows and bullets shattering the plant's crystalline stems and glass leaves. As the gardens died, the tinkling of the fragments produced an uncanny resonance; an unnatural timbre that reminded people of screams. It was only later that the symbiosis between plant and ghost was elucidated and the lament set in.

A triptych of portraits went up on a display cabinet, a nascent mirror of the ancestral shrine. Hao Ming had not yet brought a pot to burn joss sticks for the dead, and the abduction of one percent of the world's population by the Preservation Society had robbed them even of the dignity of a physical farewell. There were no bodies to be burned or buried, only the strange creeping of the alien plants. That, and the ghosts.

The government had allocated this flat to him with scant information about the previous occupants. The garden in the bedroom was intact, so the ghosts had not been evicted by violence. Not every garden had ghosts, although evidence suggested that gardens all started with them. Some ghosts, for reasons still not fully understood, just faded. Not for the first time, Hao Ming wondered if that was what had happened to his family.

But Hao Ming was certain there was a ghost still in this flat; there was always a steaming cup of coffee under the coffee machine, the overflow spilling onto the counter and dripping onto the floor, dried coffee staining the tile in a creeping Rorschach pattern. Netflix would channel surf when he wasn't looking and the lights would go on and off to match a stranger's circadian rhythm.

Even after a week, Hao Ming had not spent much time in the bedroom, but now he wandered back in, where the flower patch sang as it slowly grew its crystalline leaves and petals. Years after the occupants had been taken, he could still make out the outlines on the bed where the plants had first taken root. The plants were the most obvious signs of the cataclysm that had befallen the world. The Preservation Society had executed the heist in a matter of hours, an alien force of such technological advancement that governments had still been puzzling over sensor data when the crisis struck, and the Society was gone again before the scale of the damage was known, leaving nothing but tears and a single message in their wake.

Everybody had heard the message at least once in the chaotic days and weeks after the event. A data packet of strangely dense encoding, the artistry of which still puzzled scientists. For a few hours, the message had been broadcast on repeat across all channels, from old analogue radio to air-gapped networks. On it, the Preservation Society said they would take, without permission, without forgiveness, a sample of every sentient species they came across, but would leave a gift to soften the parting. People remembered the message in fragments, like a half-lost dream. No one could say for certain what the aliens looked like or sounded like, any impressions were vague and contradictory. The only thing the recipients agreed on was the message. The substance of it defied scientists, stills only captured static, analysis of the audio only output white noise.

Whatever the Preservation Society was, their values were vastly different from those of humankind. There was no pattern in the selected abductions. Rich and poor alike were taken, with no discernible pattern. The bed in his new home reminded Hao Ming of returning to his silent apartment the night the Preservation Society struck, looking at beds bearing strange silicaceous growths whose beauty could not outweigh the panic rising in his throat.

The news had eventually said that the plants produced a sustained bioelectric field that allowed for the long-term existence of self-propagating signals of untold complexity. Commentators stripped the jargon from the science and added a little conspiratorial seasoning — the alien gardens were haunted by those that had been taken. It might have surprised the aliens to know that their gift of functional immortality was first greeted with fear, confusion, and in short order, violence. Then, the ghosts began to talk. Haltingly, at first, as they relearned how to interact with the world. Each ghost had their own journey back to the world of the living. Some never made it. Hao Ming's original home remained frustratingly silent, more like a tomb than a home. He had laid out funereal offerings to his family, hoping to lure them towards the material world. But doubt had set in, and more than once he thought to smash the plants sprouting from where his family had lain in slumber. Instead, he left, though the only opportunity for housing was another abandoned flat, another modern sepulchre.

Hao Ming stood now over someone else's bed, again tempted to violence. Instead, he shifted over to the bedside table and placed the wedding portrait face down before leaving the room.

This is how we stay alive: If we are not anchored, we will drift free.

Panic was a physiological response, a flood of neurochemicals provoking changes in body chemistry: the muscles tightened, the breathing quickened, the stomach contracted. A ghost did not have the benefit of these, only a disembodied feeling of doom as a stranger approached their garden with violence in his hands and murder in his eyes. This stranger turned away at the last minute, shifting Jeff's wedding photograph on the table.

Even sighing in relief was a pleasure denied to ghosts, but Jeff felt tension ease all the same.

He followed the new tenant to the living room and paused with him at the small memorial to the other man's family. A plaque at the bottom of each portrait marked out a year familiar to Jeff. At least he had one thing in common with his new roommate.

It was not possible for Jeff to right his wedding picture, even if he felt his existence solidify the nearer he was to the garden. Once, he could have traced where he and Pris had lain on their last night from the outline of the leaves, in the curl of stems over the bedsheets. Now, the plants were rampant, with their strange hum, and that last physical reminder of Pris was gone. All he had was the memory of her and her quiet smile, saying that she had to go first and that he could follow when the time was right. There was little he could have done to stop her as she stepped out of their flat, away from the nourishing field of the growing garden and into dissolution.

They'd argued about it before, while watching the news about ghosts disappearing. They frequented forums populated by the recently disembodied, even held down some gig work doing speech to text transcription until those opportunities dried up. Three fates awaited the ghosts. The gardens could be, and had been, destroyed. They were hardy but not invulnerable. They did not burn well, but like all things made of glass, they shattered on impact. Not only did assailants report the plants screaming, but even faraway gardens keened and scintillated in distress when one of their own was murdered. There were no documented observations of what happened to ghosts during the violence, save that they did not survive it.

Second, the gift of the gardens was not permanent. Like all living things, they needed nourishment. Laborious observation distinguished the gardens that thrived and those that withered along with their ghosts. Governments, organisations, and religions all over the world had boiled the mysteries down into insipid catechisms like the one Jeff and Pris had gotten, because what fed the gardens was a ghost's attachment to the world. Stories abounded about ghosts who, despite proximity to their gardens, faded all the same, and their gardens withered not long after.

A third way out was whispered about in internet forums frequented by ghosts. A ghost could just leave their garden. Nearby gardens could still sustain them, but eventually the ghosts would find the edge of the gardens' succour, whether it be at their doorstep or miles from home. Beyond that lay dissolution. Speculation was rampant amongst the ghosts that escaping the gardens was not a death sentence. Pris had bought into these theories unequivocally, that the Preservation Society had left humanity the gardens, but the gift was only a stepping stone. Debates between Jeff and Pris grew heated, blossoming into shouting matches. Perhaps they would have fought, but ghosts could no more touch each other than they could the physical world. Words alone hadn't been enough to stop Pris, and his last memory of her was of her fading as she left the flat that imprisoned them, disappearing like motes of dust on the morning breeze.

With Pris gone, Jeff struggled to maintain his connection to the garden, throwing himself into the banal rituals of daily life to cling onto existence. Grief, too, had a physiological component and Jeff felt guilty that his own mourning lacked the tightening of his throat and the unbidden leakage of tears.

Now, he found himself staring at the sleeping form of the intrusive tenant. He could not be perceived by the other man, but there were ways of making his presence felt, at least on anything electronic his tenant used. Some ghosts became malicious digital tricksters, getting into social media accounts, banks and worse. They were impossible to evict and rendered their homes near uninhabitable.

Jeff could have done any of those things to the interloper, but he didn't want to go down that route. Instead he just left Pris' photograph on the man's computer, with the dates of her birth and death inscribed below, save that the latter was the date of her second death, the day she had walked out the door to the sound of the garden trilling in the background.

Some days, Hao Ming couldn't even tell that his new home was haunted. There were terms of the shared rental, fixtures he couldn't move, rooms he couldn't change. He respected the ritual of morning coffee, even emptying and washing the cups after the coffee had grown cold. Industrial bleach returned the kitchen tiles to their previous insipid off-white.

Hao Ming found the picture of one of the flat's previous occupants on his computer one morning. The date stuck out. The previous occupants were ghosts, but the date of passing was much more recent.

Pricked by his conscience, Hao Ming slunk into the bedroom with the gait of a dog returning to the scene of a stolen treat or mangled cushion. He set the picture by the bedside upright again. The plants seemed to tinkle in appreciation.

Hao Ming knew there were ways to reach out to the ghosts, but his family had never gained the facility to communicate through the electronic ether. To be fair, his mother couldn't even use WhatsApp when she was alive. His wife and son, on the other hand, had been digital natives. It made their silence all the more frustrating. Not so in his new flat; the ghosts here made their presence known with the constantly refreshing picture on his computer screen.

The fittings in the flat were slowly in the process of being overwritten, a palimpsest of two lives overlapping. The bedroom was untouched. Hao Ming replaced the living room couch with a pullout and kept the study as his office. The date of the woman's passing was odd, past the date of the Preservation Society's visit. He remembered the verdant garden on the queen bed. Somehow the wife had died later. Hao Ming's hands hovered over the keyboard and then he reached out to the ghost.

Your wife, how did she go? Did she fade?
No, she left.
Ghosts can't leave their gardens.
That's right. She believed the gardens were just a stepping stone.
What do you believe?
I'm still here, aren't I? What happened to your family?
I don't know. They never reached out to me. They could be there, they could be gone.
But you left.

Yes, I did.

Then we have something in common, Hao Ming.

The first leaf fell one stormy morning before Jeff had completed his daily ritual. The garden's leaves were arranged in fibonacci spirals, their translucence shot through with veins that networked into aperiodic motifs. When the leaf bounced off the bed sheet, it shattered into identically shaped shards.

Jeff could not touch the shattered leaf, but when his finger approached the pieces, a residual charge almost made him tingle. The other leaves sighed. He'd read about the signs of a garden withering before, he'd just never thought it'd happen to him. The nearby gardens seemed to know; they'd emit a low hum, undetectable to human ears, that discomforted pets and grated on ghosts like fingers on chalkboards, crying in anticipation of death.

Pris' research had grown increasingly esoteric before she left. She had said the gardens were only the first step in the gift the Preservation Society had left behind, that the instructions were in the message. It sparked another row between them, Pris insisting that the single most consumed piece of media in the world had layers that the best scientists and worst conspiracy theorists had not yet deciphered.

"Everybody in the world has heard the message," he'd said to her.

"Only the message they've chosen to hear," she answered.

How long was the message for you, Hao Ming?

Two minutes and fifty-four seconds.

Mine was three minutes and fifteen.

Did Pris ever ask you about the difference?

She would have said I was not ready.

What does it say? The rest of the message?

That the gardens weren't the true gift. That we have to take the first step.

No ghost has ever come back from leaving a garden.

Pris once told me that the largest living organism on Earth wasn't a whale, or a tree. It was a fungus, growing under a forest, a massive network of mycelial cells, big as a city.

Like the —

Each garden knows what's happening to the other gardens. All other gardens. Not just here. Everywhere.

Even the ones back in my home?

Even those. The garden is still there, isn't it? There's a chance that your family is there.

They were quiet for years, Jeff.

Maybe your home has the same thing Pris was looking for beyond the gardens, what the Preservation Society left in their message.

What's that?

Faith.

This is how we stay alive: We never leave our gardens.

Hao Ming had left in the morning, at Jeff's insistence. He had a family to get back to, if they were still there. Jeff's assurances didn't help. He couldn't have explained how he knew people he'd never seen before were still waiting next to their garden, or how their garden had told him this. The refractions in his bedroom were particularly vibrant that morning, as though his own garden already knew. Broken rainbows danced on the walls and followed him into the living room. Hao Ming had left the front door open. Jeff wanted to see, and the sunlight beyond the threshold looked very bright indeed.

There was no way of knowing what lay beyond the sanctuaries of the gardens. In the first half of the message, the world had come away with the knowledge of the Preservation Society's gift — that the gardens gave life beyond flesh. But the second half, the part that only the few heard and even fewer acted on, that part was a reason. A reason, and a promise.

The Preservation Society did just that — they Preserved. The first precious few became ghosts, and even fewer of the ghosts could take a step beyond. Perhaps the message was more than a collection of data that bypassed comprehension. Pris had believed that the second part of the message was a test of faith. Jeff thought different, that perhaps the message itself was choosing those that were ready to hear it in its entirety. Those that were ready take that step. Jeff felt the familiar tug of his garden, anchoring him to the only existence he'd known for years. The nearer he got to the threshold, the more he felt himself stretching out, pulled taut like a sheet nailed down to his garden. It was an old fear, that the garden was the only thing keeping him alive. Not this time, only the promise of something more.

So he went forward and out and took the first step into the rest of his life.

See L. Chan's story "This is How We Stay Alive"
online at Metaphorosis.
If you liked it, leave a comment. Authors love
that!
Remember to subscribe to our e-mail updates so
you'll know when new stories are posted.

About the story

There seem to be two types of post-apocalyptic stories — the more popular one being the ones where a majority of the population has been wiped out. Or turned into vampires. Or zombies. I do like the other one — where everything on the planet has fundamentally changed in the near future. I liked the idea of ghosts in a science fiction setting — disembodied spirits but with clear rules. The resolution of the story had very much to do with Dan Simmon's *Hyperion Cantos*, it's resolved in a very similar way! The story was originally written from a single point of view, but I went for the split point of view in the end, trying to show that the resolutions for each character were equally valid. At the end, the story is very much about connections and letting go — the characters have to do both through the course of the story.

A question for the author

Q: Where do you write?

A: I used to write everywhere I could lug my tablet, but since I downgraded it, it's all been writing at home on the PC.

About the author

L. Chan hails from Singapore. He spends most of his time wrangling a team of two dogs, Mr Luka and Mr Telly. His work has appeared in places like *Clarkesworld, Translunar Travellers Lounge, Podcastle, the Dark,* and he was a finalist for the 2020 Eugie Foster Memorial Award. He tweets inordinately @lchanwrites and can be found on the web at lchanwrites.wordpress.com

A word about Evan Marcroft

Evan Marcroft first came to our attention in 2018, and we published his story, "The Little G-d of Łódź" on 02 November of that year. It's a story of Nazis and war and golems and sacrifice that's dark but still uplifting.

He appeared again in *Metaphorosis* not long after, with "The Color of My Home is Red Like an Apple" on 29 March 2019, pondering just what it means to have faith, and how that intersects with choice. Things took a distinct turn toward funny with "Devilish Calliope and the Ungrooviest Apocalypse" on 14 August 2020.

Just before that, Evan had participated in of our most demanding anthologies to date, *Reading 5X5 x2: Duets.* While the first *5X5* anthology asked 25 authors to write from just five prompts, the *x2* anthology asked five authors to write with *each other* — four collaborative and one solo story, all in a short period. Evan's stories, "Lambs Fight to Die" (solo), "Boro Boro" (with J. Tynan Burke), "Snakeheart" (with Douglas Anstruther), "Titanotheosis" (with David Gallay), and "The Blood Dance of Ape and Mouse") with L'Erin Ogle, were among the most inventive, with wild and memorable worlds that I'd love to see more of — particularly the weird and wonderful world of "Lambs Fight to Die", with its furniture of zombie body parts, and the bizarre and majestic "Titanotheosis" with its constructed gods fighting for dominance.

Here's his latest for *Metaphorosis*, "The Bloodless Cut".

The Bloodless Cut

Evan Marcroft

I glance at the bracelet on my left wrist. *Nineteen minutes and fifty-eight seconds,* it reports. *Fifty-seven now. Fifty-six.* Meanwhile the door is dilating shut behind me until it disappears entirely, rendering the seven-by-seven-meter cell as airtight as something meant to hold monsters must be.

The room is almost entirely featureless, the bed just a pillow-less slab of the same impervious substance as the floor. No faucets or drains either; I wonder idly where water comes from, where waste goes. Light emanates directly through the walls and with no shadow in which to hide, the room's ghost haunts in plain sight. She sits upon a backless stool in the geometrical center of the room facing a vertical blue stripe on the wall that creates the illusion of a window-slit. The pale arc of her back resembles that of a flesh-tearing fang with a ratty black tuft skewered on the tip. Her gossamer shift conceals nothing, not her rippling alabaster ribs nor their dermatitic rosettes.

Fifty-three, fifty-two...

This dwindling time is the last we'll ever spend together.

"Doctor Nichirei."

Her voice is a dungeon hinge shedding four months of rust.

"It's good to see you. I'm so happy my teacher came to visit."

Teacher. I want suddenly to bite my fingers, but I've had years to master the urge.

"I wish I could say the same," I reply. "On both accounts."

"Is it done then? Has the Peacock finally scratched the Fox's eyes out?"

"It was inevitable, once the Fox lost its teeth." I adjust my spectacles. "The word is unconditional surrender, as of two weeks ago. The rebel princes are all in custody or dead. This madness is done.”

“And yet an Emperor still sits the Sapphire’d Chair,” the prisoner muses. “But then, I long suspected that would be so. You were always so stubborn, Doctor.”

The shadow of an accusation chills me.

“Just before you arrived, a guard gave me this to drink.” Her hand swings out, holding a paper cup too small to choke on. “Was it poison? It tasted sweet.”

The empty phial in my pocket smolders against my thigh.

“No. But you are to be executed today.” A choice made above even my lofty reach. Were it my call, this woman would fall into a gap in history from which she could never climb out.

Water on white canvas. The news soaks spotlessly into her. “That’s good. I can almost hear them now — the public that is, out there baying for my death. Seeing it is the most important thing. The spectacle *always* is. The spectacle is all.”

How did she know? I tell myself that anyone could have guessed a crowd of thousands surrounded the Citadel of Scales, all jostling to witness the moment the guillotine falls, but nothing is certain with this woman. Even these walls can’t guarantee they'll hold her even when all logic says they should.

I turn over my palm. A silver tablet, pillowed in callused pink corduroy. A gentle toss. Halfway to the prisoner it unfurls propeller arms that lift it into a stable orbit. Her ear twitches towards its fey hum.

"What's this? An autoquill?"

"His Perpetual Will has commanded your final words be documented for historical and scientific purposes."

I can't help but flinch as she swivels to face me with a motion so smooth and unsignaled it is almost mechanical. Four months of solitary confinement are etched invisibly into this woman. Her bun is solidly black where my curls run with autumn colors. She seems too young for this aftermath-era, also unlike me, my lines deep as grief.

"That's not the Emperor I know," frowns Vasani Stirio. "What combination of words is he hoping to hear, pray tell?"

"Everything," I say simply.

Our wars lousy with criminals who would rather not be infamous.

Some of the best worked for me.

You'll find them hardly the cackling villains that popular conception make of men like them. They're the ones in the backgrounds of the declassified photographs, the little ones with the shiny spectacles and soft, nervous faces. *I was only following orders*, they invariably plead until the guillotine cuts them off. History remembers them with a kind of smirking scorn, as if their real sin was a dearth of pride. That is not Vasani Stirio now and it wasn't her then.

No student of mine ever made excuses.

She arrived at the Quintelzean Empire Military Defense Institute a serious, almost solemn scientist, deferential to her superiors, a reliable volunteer for undesirable chores — the same as all the bland brains I employed. My subordinates all came from the top academies and I assumed her story was formulaic. I scarcely noticed her then. Just another set of hands to help screw together my grand designs.

For years that was the way of things. It wasn't until our hands met within the innards of the same town-flattening rocket that I noticed how quickly Vasani had climbed to where I was. As we scrubbed our greasy hands at the same sink, I saw that her fingertips were chewed to rubbery coarseness. And the following month, when word reached us that our rocket had transmuted an entire enemy battalion into radioactive bauxite sculptures, she spoke only to suggest how the effect-radius could be expanded, tugging at her gloved fingers all the while.

It was then I knew I needn't ask her story.

Your reflection remembers where you've been.

"Care to sit? There's plenty of floor."

"I don't have long," I say. *And it's easier to run from a standing position.* I'm only realizing now that I really am in here with Vasani, sharing her air, her proximity. There is a circle of red paint in a three-foot radius around her stool. While she remains within the circle my safety is guaranteed outside of it, but that assumes anything is guaranteed near Vasani Stirio.

"Suit yourself," she shrugs. "How *have* you been, Mirchelle? Is your littlest well? I understand young Vasri endured an aerocopter accident some months ago."

My breath catches at the sound of my son's name between her teeth. How does she know about that? How, after everything I did to keep my son invisible throughout the war. My hand tightens involuntary around the phial in my pocket, almost crushing it. I force myself to let go. What's done is done, what's known is known, and I have eighteen minutes left to work with.

"I'm not here to reminisce."

"If you won't answer my questions, why should I answer yours?"

"I've been authorized to administer force."

She once described my stare as surgical. *You take people apart with a scalpel and forceps.* Now I wish I could swat away her gaze as it probes with implements beyond my imagining. "That's not you," she says disapprovingly. "Don't tell me you're still the Emperor's little do-anything device after everything that's transpired? Did that war we fought teach you nothing?"

The autoquill whirs needily in every small silence. What I say next I say as quietly as truth must sometimes be.

"His Perpetuity the Emperor is a lion and a sun. I speak only with his voice."

It's where I place the stresses that makes Vasani's eyes sparkle with convincing mirth. I have also watched soldiers cackle as they die. I have difficulty interpreting expressions, but I have rarely missed the knack. Why would I? The face speaks a language that means nothing.

"Your master will get what he wants, but it will be of no use to him."

"Why?" I demand, suddenly suspicious.

That smile. That awful, scalpel-cut smile. I've given her the tool to slice me open and do with me as she pleases. I catch my fingers creeping towards my lips and force them into a fist. I don't like that she knows this, but if I am to ever understand what killed Vasani Stirio and came to live inside her skin, I must endure her, as all her victims did before me.

"Because what I do is no method that can be taught," she purrs. "Rather, it is a height of craft reachable only through a supremacy of will far beyond your Emperor. But you, Doctor Nichirei... I suppose you may understand."

A finger stands up on her hand, translucent around the edges where the light perforates its meatless skin and blurs the shadow of her bone. My foreboding doubles and redoubles again when two more join it. "The perfect torture requires the mastery of three impossible cuts," she says.

"Let us discuss the first."

The Unhealing Cut

Vasani Stirio vanished a week after the Schism that split the Empire in two. A month before the war began in-earnest. *Abducted by the enemy,* was what I first suspected.

I would only learn the truth once the Screaming Ships came home.

The first few clashes were a series of successes for the Emperor's Peacocks. We smashed the Foxes at Thoracic Ridge, at the Glass Plains, drove that cabal of rebel princes across the River Quyle, all within the first few weeks. The Foxes fought cleverly, but my brain was itself a military asset. The state-phasing ghostrounds I provided made a joke of enemy body armor, while my magma-mortars flooded emplacements with fire. The campaign proved taxing even so, but if we could just push through and end the war fast, we could spare those soldiers yet outside our firing range. Then came the so-called Just Offensive, our chance to liberate the rebel-held Chelenon and unseat the Foxes from the region. The town, however, sat beneath a fearsome gunfort, and it threatened a grueling siege.

A siege that never came to be.

The night before our assault began, soldiers began complaining of ants infesting their bedrolls. They went to their medics reporting insect bites and were given standard-issue salves, which did not work. Within the hour, itching progressed to burning. Within two hours, that burning worsened to a pain so unbearable that men begged for fewer limbs. Dawn broke over a siege-camp in chaos. Six in ten had been stung, and no combination of painkillers, styptics, or sedatives could ease their agony.

The true horror, however, lay dormant for weeks, waiting for those soldiers to be packaged home aboard what came to be called the Screaming Ships, where our best military scientists could only scratch their heads. I examined the victims myself, ears muffled against a wailing that only a hacksaw could quiet, and reached the same conclusion which the following years would prove true. The pain was permanent.

Those bitten would howl forever.

The Emperor's war-ministers were in a fury, partly of fear, partly envy. *How*, they demanded. *How was it done? How could we do the same?* Specimens recovered from Chelenon offered few answers. Magnifying only a few degrees beyond their chitin revealed a labyrinth of manipulated genetics impenetrable even to me. But that mystery was, itself, an answer.

Biofabrication was never *my* specialty.

Some passengers of the Screaming Ships still live. In hospitals they reside now, kept in medical comas from which they are woken for mere minutes of the year to plead for sleep or death — confirmation that what they suffered not be forgotten or escaped. A man stung on the finger could lose a finger. A man stung on the leg could lose the leg. A man stung on the breast? That man was damned alive. Our armies never returned to

Chelenon; the ground there was cursed, and the only shots fired there were suicides. While I toiled in my laboratory devising weapons that could terminate life ever more efficiently, Vasani Stirio had already determined not to fight a war at all.

"Would you prefer I had bombed them, Doctor Nichirei?"

Her expression betrays only infinite patience. She will die waiting for the answer she covets.

Sixteen minutes forty.

"Yes," I admit under time's duress. "I would have preferred that you bombed them."

"Would you have done it?"

Monster that she is, of course she craves more. "I've never once made a tactical decision," I begin, "but... you know I try and speak with soldiers returning from the front. I listen to their stories, what they tap out on my hand with the fingers they have left. A life you cannot live is worse than hell, Vasani. You replaced everything those soldiers might have felt with fire. I don't see why you couldn't make it quick."

The corner of her mouth twitches up and her eyelids droop. *I'm sorry, that must have been difficult*, is what I'd normally trust that face to say. "That would have been a waste," Vasani says, almost tenderly. "A body can be written off in a ledger. Numbers never persuaded anyone. Is that not why you meet with soldiers? Because their words say more than the official report ever could? You can chew if you like, by the way."

It's a very her thing to say. Both mocking, caring, neither, and both. I dig nails into my palms in a substitute stimulus. "Life is the best teacher."

"And life taught you to fear pain before death, but remember: pain is the *younger* monster of the two, born only when death for the first time ever *failed*. You taught me so much but you never appreciated suffering for the resource it is. Tanks and artillery are only vehicles for the delivery of pain, and less — the threat of it, the execution of it, proving our stockpiles are full... that is how castles fall and monuments rise. Before there were words, there were rocks and sharp sticks. Knuckles across the eyes. *Do what I say or else.* Speech is a useful abstraction, but torture is and always will be humanity's first language. Do you disagree?"

Sixteen minutes, thirty-eight seconds.

"War too is an abstraction," she continued. "It is the democratization of torture, but the objective remains the same. We're always looking for ways to extract consequence without dirtying our things, even understanding that the cost will always be brutality. I simply did away with these unnecessary abstractions and returned to our species' roots."

There's a sickness percolating through my guts. I am nineteen again, watching my professor spread a fetal piglet's numbles to show how they work. *Here is the liver. Here is the spleen. Here is the heart. Remember to take careful notes.* "You can't honestly believe what you did was preferable to death."

"Only when death manifests as warfare. The weapons you and I designed reaped soldiers by the thousands yet took only a moment's hurt from each. How was our foe to fear that? A flash of agony, then peace? Do you take a sip of wine and toss the bottle? That young dumb men still strapped on boots and rush against your inventions should tell you something

Doctor Nichirei. War is wasteful." She shakes her head. "Were one to transmute the body's total potential suffering instantly into energy it would wipe the Emperor's palace off the map."

I hope she's speaking colorfully, not theoretically. I've seen too much of Vasani's technology not to be wary. "You and I both sought to extract the greatest consequence from the smallest bloodshed," she says, "but only I dared approach it. Only I dared touch the sublime."

My fingertips are itching furiously.

"What you fear more than pain and death alike is perpetuity. A body can endure unimaginable suffering but the mind dreads forever so badly that it chooses instead to age. Only once you accept the infinite suffering within can you take the first step towards where I stand now."

Sixteen minutes, eleven seconds.

"The First Cut is the Unhealing Cut. The wound that does not close. Pain is the power source you turn to when all others are exhausted, and when released it must be explosion of consequence enough to lay armies flat on the ground. This you saw for yourself at Chelenon."

"And in the survivors who begged for death in my arms," I counter. "A simple smartfiber nanomesh added to our soldier's fatigues gave our soldiers no reason to dread a bug-bite ever again. I finished the design in a night. The next month we pushed into Fox territory from further north and seized the Kruholidon Mountain Manufactory Complex. This 'cut' of yours came to nothing."

Vasani's lips purse. "Maybe so. But remember, Doctor: I had only just begun my journey."

In two motions, hip and spine, she ratchets upright, and I take an unthinking step back towards the door. *Fifteen minutes*, my bracelet assures me. *Fourteen now, and fifty-nine seconds.*

Vasani smiles. "Be at ease. You're perfectly safe. But that reaction, yes, that is... illustrative. For fear must come before the cut, doctor. The flesh must know it is to split. That must be its dreaded destiny, and for that your cut must violate all boundaries. Physical, spatial, temporal. You must make an idiot stroke capable of slitting the impossible."

The Untethered Cut

I would only learn exactly how the Foxes swayed Vasani to their side in the war's aftermath, from documents recovered at one of her secret laboratories. The covert politics aren't terribly relevant. Knowing my student, I spared little thought for the resources those rebel princes offered. I only ever stared at the white blanks between the lines. What she never asked for in words, but received nonetheless. Always were Vasani's reasons her own, and never put to paper.

It wasn't long after Chelenon that the Emperor ordered a new offensive, this time into the Valley of Ten Lakes. If successful, it would have brought our forces practically to the Fox's stoop, but that basin between the mountains was a fungal forest riddled with swamps, sinkholes, and blinding miasmas. Worse, the Foxes had seeded the area with guerillas who knew secret trails and spider-holes from which they could nip bites off our lumbering platoons.

With the memory of the Screaming Ships still fresh, I designed respirators that adapted to the marshland's infinite poisons, built exoskeletons that could weather envenomed bolts and parasitic larvae. Thus equipped, the Imperial 31st Scouting Brigade began to make headway again. By the third night of the third month, our forces had very nearly cleared the valley.

My mistake was thinking Vasani would repeat herself.

History is smashed in that godforsaken valley. There is no complete record left of what exactly happened to the twenty-seven soldiers of the 31st who vanished into that malarial hell. Progress halted as the fragmented unit dredged the bogs, finding nothing. Either the swamps had swallowed them, or something that digested bone and body armor.

Then, six days and sweltering nights later, the Imperial 31st leapt awake at a screaming amongst the trees. Not animal; too familiar. There came a frantic splashing, and hard, scarred soldiers fumbled for their guns. They waited tensely for the wailing shadows to tell them what was wrong. Then at last, a figure burst out of the reeds and into the firelight. A shambling corpse it seemed, green with algae and embarrassed with bug-bites, until suddenly it raised its hands and called for help.

They called it a miracle that all twenty-seven escaped. None could quite recall how exactly; even their time in captivity was a nauseating blur. What mattered was that they were alive, unharmed, and homesick. All twenty-seven were sent once to the capitol to receive a hero's welcome. I intercepted them before they got that far. For weeks I subjected them to every test possible, yet for the life of me found nothing amiss. The men remained in good spirits, eager to hold their children again.

It wasn't until they were safe amongst their families that Vasani's trap sprung.

There had to be some sort of hormonal trigger buried insidiously deep in their genes, primed to spring when the poor men were at their happiest. It caught some of them at dinner, some in congress, others as they dandled their daughters on their knee and promised they'd never leave home again.

It would have begun with an invasive squirming beneath the skin. I know now that was their circulatory system uprooting and moving into a new position. That squirming would have become a burning as every connective subdermal fiber in them began to creep like a million millipede feet. How they must have fought their twisting, knotting flesh, trying to push their drifting eyes back into place, to keep their ears from crawling into new positions, all uselessly. They could only watch as their skin blanched with a grave-shroud complexion, and as their eyes, noses, and mouths gravitated together into new configurations too petite for their skulls. If they kept their wits they thought of knives — that or hot irons to cauterize the creep of features — but nothing could stop it, much less reverse it, and when it was done, the children they'd longed to hold looked up into twenty-seven gibbering facsimiles of Vasani Stirio.

By morning, the Empire knew monsters were real.

What can some nanomesh do against that? What can any armor do? What can trenches and bunkers and miles of distance and sloshing seas do? What can they do against a knife that can descend anywhere, upon anyone?

Thirteen minutes, thirty seconds.

"You're chewing, doctor."

She's right. I spit my fingers out, jam them in my pockets. "And you're mad."

Vasani tilts her head, a quizzical look left incomplete— now that I think of it, I can't remember when she last blinked. "That's a funny thing to say. Had your forces cleared the valley it would have meant a bloody battle. Your soldiers ran home instead of into our bayonets. Most of them, at any rate."

"They ran into mental wards," I hiss through gritted teeth. "They ran from something they couldn't escape, that *you* set upon them."

"They ran off with their futures ahead of them, Doctor Nichirei. That's more than His Perpetuity offered when he ordered them into the meat-grinder."

My every fibril tenses when Vasani begins to pace. Her bare feet suck softly at the concrete, as close to the red circle as they can without touching it. Does she know she's frittering away my time, her time, our time? A wormier thought: is this a ploy? "You still had to capture all those soldiers you warped. You had to lay your hands upon them to ruin them." *Hands that once met in the guts of a rocket.* "How can you say you achieved this second Impossible Cut?"

"Turn it around, doctor. They were not my subjects; they were my *instruments*, and through them I reached the Empire's heart. That was where I made my incision." Her finger is upon her breast, an untrimmed nail digging into her flesh, making it blush. "The Untethered Cut is the cut that appears anywhere. On any flesh, on any continent, past any defense. Sons, daughters, fathers, sisters, lovers, enemies — when you can perform this cut you will have transcended the boundary of distance, and the world will never feel safe again."

"Is that what you call an efficient use of pain? What did you even achieve besides misery?"

She stops her pacing suddenly and so does my pulse. All the peaks in my biorhythm flatten into a silent line. The core of human fear is the unknown. That is what Vasani is now, quite deliberately I think. Some crimes decouple ability from the limitations of flesh. That is why I flush cold when she doesn't blink. Why I start at every small motion she makes.

There is no knowing what that motion might make of *me.*

"You know you're perfectly safe, Doctor Nichirei," she grins, her point eloquently made.

"No-one will be until your head rolls," I throw back, suppressing a shudder.

"You're right. I showed them their Emperor was neither a lion nor a sun. That he could not protect them nor save them from what lurks in the dark."

"But it wasn't enough," I'm quick to remind her. Not for the Emperor's honor — I retch at the notion — but for spite. "In spite of everything you did, the war continued."

Ten Minutes.

One second.

The Unique Cut

When I think back upon the Schisms I imagine a no-man's land overcast by two shadows, but that's the bias of first-person memory. All I did was pack men into tanks. The real war was between

Vasani Stirio and His Perpetuity, the Emperor of All Quintelzéa.

That man did not feel what his body felt; that much I can't argue. Princes of the imperial family are born into a complex of nested seraglios known as the Tesseract Halls, at the center of which a developing child cannot possibly catch a whiff of the real world. Hence, his war-verve remained a straight line while public enthusiasm dropped at a sharp angle. It didn't seem to matter what new thing to fear she discovered — waves of dissent met riot shields and broke. Magtrams kept freighting fresh recruits towards the front and returning only empty seats. All of this meant that a war we should have lost continued, and Vasani's tactics continued to evolve.

Nevertheless, the two fed into one another. The Emperor's only response to the newest atrocity was rageful escalation, in turn prompting some of Vasani's worst, most ingenious inventions. In response to his encircling of Grivbaénk, she unveiled the Finger Eater and sent his men into a rout. At the Hydrokloric Falls, she presented a piece dubbed the Living Skeleton. Two in ten live witnesses took their own lives. Amidst the siege at

Steampike Castle, Vasani somehow spirited away a senior officer and reinterpreted him as something papers called the Tear-Stained Puzzlebox, which remains tragically unsolved to this day. There were others examples I could recall — Vasani always was a restless tinkerer — but some memories go into you like shrapnel, and it's safer to leave them be.

Steampike Castle still fell, but the poor officer's fate was a tipping point back at the capital.

Vasani Stirio seemed impossible to capture. The woman was a ghost haunting abandoned labs full of half-baked horrors. She'd transformed herself into a magical evil that could snatch up anyone, anywhere, and do anything to them. When citizens no longer felt safe in their homes, they took to the streets. Soldiers stopped enlisting and began deserting in greater numbers. Curfews and public executions scaffolded everyday life in the same brutal military logic that held the war together.

Faced with domestic mayhem, the Sapphire'd Throne elected to ignore it. For all of the above, the Foxes were losing. Vasani's creations strangled public morale, but they couldn't make up for quantumflame rockets or my inversion mines, nor topple the implacably stomping trenchwalkers I devised to trample enemy emplacements. I built the Emperor all the excuse needed to continue as he always had, but only I seemed to notice that Vasani's methods were growing more meticulous, less bloody, though my warnings went unheard. All I could do with all my power was tighten the screws on the war-machine. Days and nights spun into a crepuscular blur as I worked myself to insomniac extremes devising new technologies, more powerful weapons.

I must have believed that by fine-tuning my craft I could eliminate all but that one miraculous invention that, with just the touch of a button, would instantly neutralize Vasani Stirio. Surely it was somewhere in my imagination.

That was my naivete: not realizing Vasani believed something similar.

"Originality," I say. "That's your third ideal."

I'm against the wall now. I have to sit and hold my knees. It's that or bite myself. "People always adapt to suffering. Souls scab over if not freed. Negative feedback loops. You know what I mean. Nerve boredom." I'm rambling as I do when overstimulated. It's better than chewing. "Keep calm carry on. Keep calm carry on. That's what we're coded to do. And to get around that, you issued yourself a challenge: never to make the same cut twice."

It's hard to look at her now. I don't know what I'm seeing. The mind I glimpse is vast and tentacular. Instead I look down.

Seven minutes, nineteen seconds.

"We live with the wounds that don't kill us," she says approvingly. "Even when they bleed and bleed and bleed. And wherever it might be made, one little scratch is just that. A scratch. And so I set off towards a third Impossible Cut. If the Untethered Cut is liberated from space, the Unique Cut transcends the past. It is the cut that never repeats and therefore cannot be anticipated."

She reaches so easily into my complexities. It's true. I was only ever reacting to Vasani. I built weapons to sink thundercruisers and turn hostiles to glass, but in retrospect I was repeating the same old stratagem. The only one I knew. "And meanwhile I was complacent."

"Yes. But luckily for you, I failed."

"What?"

Vasani spreads her hands. "No matter what I did, I couldn't reach the Emperor. I fell just short of infinite. And meanwhile that mind of yours trampled on like a town-leveling juggernaut. Now look at us. You are still my teacher, Doctor Nichirei. In the end, I could never best you."

With an oh well sort of shrug she turns her back. "Tell his Porcine Perpetuity whatever you please. It won't do him any good. In the end, it didn't help me either."

I wait, but her silence goes on and on. Is that it?

I glance at my bracelet.

No, we aren't done.

Five minutes.

"The war may not have stopped," I say, rising shakily to my feet. "But... neither did you. And you would never fight a battle you couldn't win. There must be something more at work. This third cut... It isn't really one cut, is it? It's every cut you make, an endless creative challenge, no — a very finite narrowing of both technique and possibility to the eventuality that no cut can be made at all.

You could have re-used your ever-stinging ants or given everyone in the capital your face, but you didn't. Even when it would have saved your life. Instead you chose always to innovate no matter what, to push the boundaries of your craft past the borders of known science..."

The autoquill whirs closer as if hanging on my every word.

"And yet," I continue. "A certain theme runs through your methods. It was present from the beginning; I just didn't see it until now. For a handful of bug-bites you turned the tide of a siege. You lent your face to the nightmares of millions without a single death. But your victims were never actually your victims — you let that much slip yourself. It was all about making wives weep and children wake up screaming at the memories of their fathers, yes, but also about learning, no — elimination. The Unique Cut isn't a peak, it's a method hidden in a method, a hidden path to — to —"

Silence again, but for the subaudible dribbling of time out of the world.

"—There is a fourth Impossible Cut, isn't there?"

My question throbs out into her cell's white void. Bare feet shuffle on cold stone.

Vasani's smile makes me remember when our bitten fingers first touched within the innards of a rocket. Hers are eyes that say, *I am feeling what you feel, remembering what you remember.*

What you see in me is what I see in you.

"After all this time," she murmurs. "You are still my teacher."

The last time we met was not the last time we spoke.

"Why do we aim shells at armies?"

My kitchen. The yellow table. The purpling evening through the window. The lime-green tiles above the countertop flecked red from my cutting board. *Klat.* My cleaver whacks the head off a plucked fieldfowl, and blood helpfully leaves the body. A pot simmers on the island stove behind me, salivating for meat. *She* sits over the counter beyond it, smeared by steam.

"Why not aim them at kings? Wouldn't that save everyone a lot of trouble?"

To this day I am not sure why she asked. From where I stand on the autistic spectrum, it is hard for me to read the currents that move individuals along. The face is beautiful beyond scrutiny. I understand people better in aggregate. When a population smiles, it is easier for me to understand why, but Vasani was always, in every regard, alone.

"Kings," I told her, "are hard to reach."

Klat klat klat. The bird spills open in fatty pages.

When I was seven, I tell her, my family was displaced from a kingdom that no longer exists. The old king died and his nephew came next to sit the throne, though ill he fit it, a sneering boy-tyrant who believed a boy's war would make him a man. *A king is his country's dignity.* When they drag him before a greater king and defile him with bayonets, what does that make us?

I reach for vegetables next, ripe and sweating.

Three years I spent barefoot on a mass resettlement march to a barren corner of the Empire. The harsh road took my younger brother first. A soldier's warning-shot killed my mother's leg, and when father's heart gave up on carrying her, she gave up herself and let the endless procession swallow her. Two sisters went on until the soldiers took the elder, never to be seen again. Only two blackened feet and a hard-won certainty reached my new home: that if on the first day of war we had been annihilated completely, we would have at least all gone together. For a time I dreamed of a magical bomb.

"A magical bomb," she murmurs thoughtfully. "One that kills only kings, hm?"

Done. I take my cutting board to the salivating pot. *Hiss.* The broth foams with relish.

The fact is this: the nation is a body. The king is the brain and the hands are his legions. Another fact: when threatened, the brain reflexively puts its hands in harm's way. You've seen it, that instinct manifest. For the sake of survival the brain will sacrifice everything but itself. The head is always the last to die.

"Tut. That's a broken metaphor. The 'hands' are their own beings. Should they not be spared?"

When possible, yes, but it rarely is so. I remind her that the enemy is a body too. They deserve everything that we do, but if we must fight them anyway for whatever stupid reason then let us make it as bloodless as possible. Bloodless, and brief for all involved."

"The mercy of overwhelming firepower," my student notes dryly.

The mercy of euthanasia, is what I say.

"Oh? When you called the enemy a body I didn't know you meant the four-legged sort."

Four-legged, four-legged. That is little Vasri sing-songing from the floor behind her as he stacks his blocks in coded columns. He loves to build things, my youngest son. I hope he turns out nothing like me. "The brain puts the hands before it," murmurs Vasani. "But... isn't hurt felt in the brain?"

As she said, it is a broken metaphor. In the coming years, I'll wish that I'd been more careful with it.

Broken, mama! Vasri's delighted cry heralds a *smack*, and a clatter of building blocks across the floor. I laugh and even Vasani almost chuckles as he gathers them up to begin again, and meanwhile the pot fills my kitchen with savory steam. The dish I am cooking is almost done, and it's time I laid the plates out side by side. Mine and hers, hers and mine.

There are memories that go on a shelf beside the heart.

"The Unhealing Cut extracts the fullness of pain but leaves an unsightly mark. The Untethered cut is free to strike anywhere, but still requires the analogue passage of edge through flesh. The Unique Cut hurts like the first you ever felt, every time, but some cannot be cut by knives alone. Some are too thick in hide *and* head. But there is a cut that does not parse flesh. A cut that leaves no wound at all."

The torturer's hands flower open, two lopsided albino stars. She takes one step, two, arms extending, starved tendons protracting. Her palms flatten perpendicular to the circle of red paint and mime a more solid wall into being, her fingertips all but indenting from pressure. My gaze lingers there.

Her hands. The few fingernails she has left are rusted chisels, but the pads beneath them are as immaculate as if she never once chewed them.

"Only when you have exhausted all other cuts will you find it," Vasani continues with a mounting grandiosity. "We must search for it amongst the vitals. Within the soul. Do you remember the Tear-stained Puzzlebox? Remember how two armies stopped to stare? That unlucky man was my instrument, and all who witnessed him my subjects. By the time the war entered its final stages I was pushing you back for a pittance of blood, while back home I was strangling your will to fight. Whatever form of torture we prefer, the goal is always to achieve maximal consequence through minimal violence. The acme of torture is simply success. It is a singularity of achievement where technique sublimates into will. When you can make a subject scream without a touch, you can do anything. Even stop a war – though in that I fell a *little* short."

Her cackle fills the room inescapably. "You told me it couldn't be done! But I did it. His hands whole, his belly-rolls unblemished, his very body *unbloodied!* Hah!" Suddenly she is shouting. "His Perpetuity will never understand! He is the sniveling, selfish monster-mind that throws its hands up before a knife, and I... I... I am the knife that loves the flesh and only cuts evil where it hurts. Where, doctor, where?"

"The brain," I finish hollowly.

"Nowhere," she corrects, and in a dizzying rush it all connects and I glimpse the sinews of logic conjoining the brilliant young woman I knew to this creature before me. I don't want it I don't want it I don't want it but her logic is so vivid in its twisted, mutilated symmetry and I am so attuned to patterns in the fabric of things visible and not that I cannot help but think as she thinks for a gut-wringing second, and I perceive the world emergent from its rampant fractalization.

"Name it, doctor. I know you can. *Name it!*"

"Name it!"

She almost seems to speak through me.

"The Bloodless Cut."

I have never known Vasani Stirio to laugh, but now she does. As with everything about her, it is a performance. Her eyelashes flutter and her cheeks pull back from her teeth like washed-out curtains revealing a display of mummified heads. Her mouth is a hole where a victim decomposed, the knife still in their back, and from it sounds a titter tinged with the sweet perfume of rot-riddled gums. All I can do is cower against the wall in absolute, electrifying dread. I was wrong to believe her immune to prison; it got into her like a cavity, rotting her from the inside. It is just too easy to forget that she is human when I shouldn't, for human is the most terrible thing that a monster can be.

Three minutes.

In the end, Vasani Stirio was not some intangible spirit of pain. There was a body there, however foxily it ran and hid. My understanding is that someone on the other side eventually grew disgusted with her and gave up her location. War can be ordinary like that.

I arrived by aerocopter at her secret compound high up in the frozen crags of Coldfire Mountain just a week after she was captured. The wind tried to rip my hair away as it fled, the sun just a neon rim along that shadow peak, almost gone. I reported to the camp commander, ate a tasteless ration in my habitat, and forged directly into Vasani's lab. While I'd advocated leveling the mountain with a bomb, the Emperor wanted it scrubbed of its every last secret, and in the end, I couldn't resist the lure either.

I was bundled against the lab's sterile chill and breathing out vaporous ghosts. A security detail went ahead of me into those dimly lit tunnels, clearing out booby-traps left for the unwary. I'd expected displays of inventive lethality, not simple explosives disarmed without casualties. They seemed almost... perfunctory. It was as if she knew she'd be found and couldn't resist giving her enemies a last tweak on the nose.

I won't relate what I found there. I can't. All I can say is this. If you twist and construe and deconstruct a living body long enough it will die, but at the point of balance between those two polarities it becomes something close to art. The soldiers found me retching in the snow outside. I might have stayed there forever had one not said, *ma'am, you should have a look at this*. They'd found a sealed room in the back of the complex, one that mysteriously unlocked at their approach.

I'll go, I said.

And... the rest?

Burn them.

I could smell it hovering around that steel door in the depths of the lab, a sweet-sour muddling of dung and disinfectant. It misted in the air as the identity beam scanned me and then turned green as it had for the guards. It was instantly plain to me that Vasani would have seen the Foxes losing, would have known she'd be captured, and would have formulated accordingly, and I knew that the wise thing to do was report that I'd found nothing. My chest was colder than the mountain air. Sometimes you can hear the future screaming the answer at you.

I'm not sure why I chose to ignore it; I couldn't have known what I'd find inside. It was like a moment I'd already lived repeating itself in the nightmare of a Mirchelle Nichirei who'd already made this mistake. My thumb brushed the door and it opened like a giftbox.

A living stink gusted from the dark within.

Vasani always knew more than she should. We both knew the Emperor wouldn't relent no matter the cost, but inexplicably she knew one other thing that I did not.

More than big meals and bloodshed, she knew the Emperor loved his wife.

Two minutes, three seconds.
"You didn't achieve a fucking thing," I manage, lest Vasani's madness swallow me whole.

Her hyenoid mirth subsides. "Oh?"

"The Emperor still bled in the end."

"That was his choice. He made the right one. Not that this brother of his is any better..."

There is an image that throbs inside my head. Sometimes softly enough that I can present a façade of normality, sometimes so loudly that it is all I can see and I must scream and scream until it subsides. It is a wound unlike any made before or after it, a cut made without puncturing the skull, a cut that will never close because it never bled to begin with.

"You didn't give him a choice," I say. "Vasani, you did the worst thing anyone has ever done."

I utter this as plainly as the fact deserves.

"Someone had to," she replies, just as matter-of-factly.

"And the Empress?"

Her expression is beatific. "Ah, you see, that is how you touch the sublime. *Even she did not bleed.*"

Vasani's head tilts slowly back and her open palms lift heavenward. "Something for nothing." She seems to shower in an imaginary light from an imaginary firmament. "The impossible, from my hands. Are you not awed? Consequence without pain; pain without a cut; a cut without blood; *blood without consequence!* This is the better way, doctor! The end of war itself! It is like a miracle! The miracle of the *Bloodless Cut!*"

Finally, the moment for the words I carried to her all these years.

"You're a monster."

The torturer's hands descend, a certain light leaving her.

"That's rich."

I look up and watch two tears make trails down her cheeks. I try to tell myself that I know better, that true or false these tears are just another act. But that's the thing about Vasani. She's human; all humans contain truths; anything she shows me *could* be real.

"Sometimes I have nightmares about the millions we might have killed together," she says. "All those children you made orphans will grow up broken, yes, but they *will grow up*. I took their pain without a knife and left them their lives!"

"Pieces of lives," I spit back at her. "Fucking stumps of lives! Stumps I gave them to try and fix what you did!"

A miserable giggle spills out of her. "And here I thought you only saw humans in deep-enough burn-pits. *I* see them for what they are. Beautiful vessels of possibility, and consequence, and love and brilliance and pain! Years you pelted me with Peacock soldiers, wasting all they could have been. How could I hurt my fellow man with such great care unless I loved them more than you?"

Then before my eyes her face warps like nightmare-stuff. Suddenly she is shrieking, spittle flecking from black gums, her eyes leaking liquid hate. "You're the monster! You, Mirchelle Nichirei! Everything I did could have come to something if not for you, who damned the world rather than stop butchering children, you barren-hearted unstoppable *steel creature!*"

On and on her frothing rage strobes over me, more than I can process, a leveling bombardment that drives me cringing into the corner. Are these emotions real? Are they fake? I cannot tell. This could all be another performance, but if not, then the worst has come to pass. Empathic overload drives my fingers to my teeth and there is pain, mine, something I can clasp to keep from being swept away.

My bracelet rattles warning against my varicose wrist.

One minute, three seconds.
One minute, two seconds.
One minute, one second.
One

The last time we spoke was not the last time we met.

Vasani reached the strike-site three hours before me, my aerocopter being delayed by malfunction. From the air the enemy warcamp seemed untouched, but this wasn't the kind of devastation you saw with a bomb. On descent I was given a rebreather to wear in case traces of our weapon still lingered on that salt-plain's paralyzed winds.

This was nothing to do with Peacocks and Foxes, I should say. This was another war, another foe.

The Schism was still weeks away.

The invading Vridic technomads were warned what would happen if they kept pushing into Empire domains. Now, they were a successful test of our newest microbial weapon. A sleepy sort of autopilot setting seemed to move our soldiers about their business, which was gathering the dead and laying them out in a flat clearing. This was common soldier work, but these bodies were difficult. They didn't drag right. They had to be carried. They were hard to look at.

Current estimate has it close to seven thousand, the supervising commissar informed me.

I thanked him for the report and asked him where Vasani was.

I lingered there to direct the organization of incoming cadavers according to my preferences, then found an empty tent where I could weep in the dark. Afterwards, I went looking for Vasani.

Tents billowed on endlessly like the sails of a fleet sunk hopelessly in the sand. Their snapping was the only sound. The first rows were empty. The latter would be soon. I found my student squatting before an open tent. I asked what she'd found. She said nothing. Venturing closer, I saw why.

Torquedust is a synthetic bacterium meant to be dispersed in cloud-form by an aerocopter. Once inhaled, it attacks the vertebral ligaments and hyper-inflames them until they cause the body to break its own neck. Instantly lethal in ninety-nine out of a hundred cases. These two were unexceptional. Comrades? Lovers? I couldn't tell; the windblown infection had caught them both in nude embrace, slipped in on the breaths they filled with one another's scent, took root, and then contorted their skulls one hundred and eighty degrees so that they last thing they saw was nothing.

I told Vasani we'd found no survivors. Every respiring thing in a miles-long tract was fatally rotated, down to the twisted lizards and the little wrenched mice.

Vasani said nothing.

I said that the enemy commander just transmitted terms of surrender. It's over.

Nothing.

It was instant for them, I said.

Then she said, *for ninety-nine in a hundred.*

A sweetly sulfurous stink reached my nose. A yellow pool was growing slowly beneath the leftmost body, a girl. My gaze traveled up a body that sagged as abandoned flesh should, going first by mistake to where her face should be —

just a skirt of ringlets there — then over to the other side, where it was now.

Blue eyes shot with blood flicked to mine. A purpled lip twitched.

In the girl's piss-puddle I glimpsed Vasani staring. Not at the bodies but at me. My wavering reflection. Waiting, it felt, for what her teacher had to say.

I take my fingers from my mouth. The taste of iron remains.

You steel creature.

And yet I bleed. Red wells plentifully from the impressions of my teeth.

This cut is not so bloodless.

Vasani is not the all-seeing demon she presents as. Infinite compassion is not something I ever thought I had. No one does, and that is right. I do not understand people very well, and those I do often disappoint me, but I can love people in their sometimes sad, sometimes beautiful mosaics. I can trust that in aggregate they suffer as I suffer, laugh as I laugh, and love as I love. Even now I wish I could trust Vasani that way. But that's what a lie does. A lie is a cut. Your world, my world — that mark there, between them. If everything that Vasani did really was to outmode me then I would be released.

It would mean that I hadn't loved a monster.

Only made one.

But...

But in me...

Unextractable by science...

The fear that this creature the government caught...

Or thinks it caught...

Is a fake and she's free right now and sharpening her knives her tools

And that fear will always be there, and that is her fault.

Fifty seconds.

"What if I told you that autoquill isn't recording?" I ask.

"What?" Her eyes pinch, then flick to the bee-buzzing machine.

"I never turned it on." I reach for it as I stand.

"Why not?" she demands hotly.

The autoquill nestles into my palm and retracts its rotos, goes still. "Emperor be damned," I say. "I wasn't going to lose this chance to speak to you one last time. But I still don't know whether I created you, or you created yourself. I don't think I ever will. What I do know is that I'll never get the truth from *you*."

I raise a finger. "Except for one thing."

"And what is that?"

"That this was never about right and wrong with you. It was about *you*. When you were about to lose, you decided to die famously. You'll go to the gallows tall and proud, where the world will see you smile as you drop and think that you were right. Battle fought with machines will become a thing of the past. There will be no peace through fear, but instead a new and crueler kind of war where battles rage across bodies instead of battlefields, all in honor of your genius. But you don't deserve that. I'm glad I killed you, Vasani."

I lift the phial from my pocket and show it to her.

Her tears have all dried up. The performance is over. Vasani confirms nothing, only stares.

"What is that?"

Many sleepless nights I guessed futilely at what had made Vasani put on fox ears. The Emperor's cruelty seems likely. His belligerence, his excesses, his pointless wars. If not, perhaps those nestled lovers lie forever in her eyes. Maybe it was what I said over dinner. Maybe it was all of that or nothing I can possibly imagine. Whatever it was, it doesn't matter now. There is a point between their most innocent and their most monstrous where nothing you know of a friend can undo what they become.

I really believed there was one invention that would defeat Vasani Stirio instantaneously. A magic bomb. I'd failed to find it; our forces took her anticlimactically with weeks of fighting left to go. I was too late to stop her. Instead, I discovered a different kind of miracle.

"This is a ferrolipid solution with a modicum of intelligence. I call it the Mnemophage."

Her eyes follow its spellbinding silver swirl.

"Once it enters the bloodstream, it is designed to seek out and kill those regions of the brain that house certain memories. The problem is that it doesn't know which memories are stored where. For it to function properly, the subject must be made to consciously recall those memories you wish to eliminate. This causes the corresponding neurons of the brain to light up, and in doing so lure the Mnemophage towards them. The process takes time."

Vasani isn't anywhere in her expression.

"How long."

"A little over twenty minutes."

Vasani screams and tries to lunge across the red paint circle. The second her fingers pierce that implicit barrier the light in the cell turns red, and segmented metal cords erupt from the wall to bind her arms and legs, pinioning her above her stool still shrieking with rage.

"Was *I* your subject, Vasani? You ruined me all the same."

Now that she's immobile, I feel safe enough to take a slow stroll around her cell.

"I don't think I was meant to see what I saw in your laboratory. That's war, I suppose. Mostly collateral damage. I always felt I was above murder, but it turns out I was really only distant from it."

Vasani tries to lunge again, but the cords hold her fast. She can only spit and snarl.

"In just a few moments you will lose yourself. All of you will be gone except the parts that did nothing wrong. An innocent woman will go to the guillotine never knowing why the world hates her. It will see what's become of her, and they'll fear to become her too."

I glance down. *Three seconds*, reads my bracelet.

Two.

One.

"All that," I say, "without a drop of blood."

The tears in her eyes blend with the froth around Vasani's defiant rictus. "You... you could have hidden what you saw, but you didn't, did you? No, no — you showed it to the Emperor because you knew I was right. You knew I was right, and you hated it! Admit it, monster: *you* should be where *I* am. We'll execute us both I say, student and teacher! Let our heads roll together!"

Such are her last coherent words. The rest is all screaming.

My head is spinning when the cell-door slams shut behind me, propelled around and around by an alarm that roars like rocket-fire. Several guards are sprinting towards me but I'm twenty minutes past their saving and drifting further into negative time with every passing second. Without much thought I fish the phial from my pocket and hold it to my eye. Not empty, in fact; a drop or two still quivers at the bottom — one for each dosage it contained.

My knees give out, and the phial tumbles from my palsying fingers. It bursts open and rolls, describing its death-arc – a silvery thumbnail obliterated by oblivious bootheels.

One guard trying to help me up, another urging me to stay down, all inaudible over the blaring klaxon. Vision dimming, head sinking. Quick: what hope did I allow myself? My assistants have the Mnemophage formula now; it's theirs to make of it what they will. Maybe a new kind of death to those in need. A more selective one, taking only what you can't bear to live with. Maybe, if I've taught them wisely, but I'll never know. A guard is pelting off, calling for help. The Emperor will soon rue my failure. He'll punish me before I die, if uncreatively. Is that what I deserve?

I'll never know that either. Not with my mirror broken.

My thoughts are elsewhere.

Broken, mama!

Hands and knees now, sinking fast. *Vasri, my son, my littlest one.* God why did Vasani have to name him? Why shine his face so brightly on the surface of my memory? The Mnemophage can't pass him now. In just a few moments I'll no longer be a mother. My son will never understand why I don't love him anymore.

I can't stop myself from screaming, a wordless plea for my next self to please hurry and be me so that she can suffer instead.

This hurts as only a bloodless cut can.

See Evan Marcroft's story "The Bloodless Cut" online at Metaphorosis.
If you liked it, leave a comment. Authors love that!
Remember to subscribe to our e-mail updates so you'll know when new stories are posted.

About the story

Hitler is boring. So is Joseph Stalin, and all the ilk of their dubious caliber. We know what kind of evil these guys are. Everyone's old dad has read a million books about them and can probably tell you the names of their childhood pets. At this point, these towering evil personalities have been so dismantled by historical mechanics both amateur and professional that every great act of monstrousness they committed can be tethered to some innocuous event opposite the point where their actions crossed over into the deliberately insidious — Hitler's being rejected from art school and so on and so on. When we peel them open we see clearly the fibers of causality that bring murderers of millions into existence. What interests me more are the great vile inexplicabilities strewn across the path towards an ideal world without seeming to have been placed there. The mysterious moai of monstrousness who seem at times to have been hurled at the world by God or whomever, sometimes at meteor speed. I'm talking about your Zodiac Killers, your bronze-age Sea People, and not even that — I'm referring to your Mengeles, whose lives seem transparent to the modern historian yet don't causally seem to amount to the era-shaping influences they become. Where do these people come from? What invisible events, what unrecorded tragedies? This story is my way of manifesting one such character into a controlled fictional space where such figures can be scrutinized safely, even if by the definition of this archetype they can never fully be understood. All we can do is take what few details we've painstakingly gleaned and make judgments of our own, for that is all history is: a patchwork of assumptions, some informed, some less so.

A question for the author

Q: What five words describe you?

A: I don't think any individual five are going to be comprehensive, but I think the five-word phrase 'this can be even weirder' is a great summary of my writing philosophy.

About the author

Evan Marcroft is a speculative fiction writer from California currently making his lair above a laundromat in the heart of Chicago. Evan uses his expensive degree in literary criticism to do menial data entry, and dreams of writing for video games, but will settle for literature instead. His works of science fiction, fantasy, and spine-curdling horror have appeared several times in *Metaphorosis* and elsewhere throughout this dark and unruly internet. Find a complete list at evan-marcroft.squarespace.com

evan-marcroft.squarespace.com, @evan_marcroft

A word about Vanessa Fog

As with L. Chan, Vanessa Fogg appeared in one of our very earliest issues, with "In Dew and Frost and Flame" on 3 June 2016, a story of lifelong love and friendship and true devotion.

Vanessa also appeared in our first anthology, *Reading 5X5*, writing from the same prompt as L. Chan, but producing a story, "Kitchen", that's similar in some ways but very different in others. Plus, it's got homely kitchen magic and turmeric-spiced potatoes in pastry.

Over the years, I've made a point of mostly avoiding books by Metaphorosis authors. I like to review what I read, and what if I don't like it? Vanessa's book, *The Lilies of Dawn,* was a convincing argument to change my practice — a beautifully written story that's rich in imagery and metaphor, and in an intriguingly conceived world to boot. I'll let you (encourage you to) discover it on your own, but it's got enchanted and malevolent cranes.

Here's her latest for *Metaphorosis*, "The Cold Inside".

The Cold Inside

Vanessa Fogg

Anna's frightened when the ghost girl first knocks at her door: a hard, frantic hammering in the still of night. Anna's alone at the lake house, surrounded by forest and water, the nearest neighbor a quarter mile away. That's why she and her husband bought the place: the splendid solitude, the embrace of dark pines, the view from a bluff that leads down to a private rock-strewn beach. They could retire here, Brian said. And Anna had imagined that retirement—still a good decade or so off—coffee on the deck, the lapping rhythm of waves, the dazzle of light on the water as they had toast and eggs. They would hike in the nearby state park, and buy fruit from roadside stands. They would spend time in the nearby charming small town with its boutiques and restaurants and gelato shop, with its single bookstore housed in a historic refurbished log cabin and filled with an eclectic selection of books and gifts. Perhaps Anna would join the book club hosted by that book store. She and Brian would join civic groups; in their leisure years they would become part of a local community as they had yet to do during their busy city lives. And each night they would have this retreat, this cottage perched above Lake Michigan, this piece of miraculously undeveloped shore: forest and dunes and the light off the water, the lake's subtle tides an underlying music in their lives.

Anna and her husband bought the place together. But now she's here alone.

The knocking comes again, harder. Anna runs to the door, peeks out through a side panel of glass. There's a woman on the porch—a young woman, a teen. She's soaking wet, a white dress plastered to her skin, dark hair streaking down her back. In the porchlight's golden glow—triggered by the property's motion detector

—Anna can see the girl's trembling blue lips.

She throws open the door.

The 'Woman in White' is a figure of ghost stories worldwide. Here in this northern stretch of Michigan, we have our own version. It's said that on a chill spring night, a teenage girl argued with her boyfriend. He broke up with her, just before a school dance or party. Distraught, she drove home alone and took a curve too fast; she plunged off the highway, off a high bluff, and into the cold waters of Lake Michigan. Her ghost haunts the region's lakeside communities, knocking on doors and trying to flag down cars on the road. She's always dripping wet.

Beware of touching her. Be especially wary if you're a young man. She's cold and still angry, and she's seeking warmth.

—from Haunted Tales and Legends of Lake Michigan's Shores, Storm Bay Press.

In the space between turning away to grab a blanket for the girl and then turning back, Anna finds the girl gone. In the entranceway is only a puddle of water, slowly spreading across the hardwood floor.

Anna is often cold. Brian used to tease her about it. He was warm—so warm. She wore sweaters, wrapped herself in blankets, and snuggled hard against him in bed. Her head tucked into the space between his neck and shoulder. The softness of flesh, the hardness of bone. His warmth warming her through. He sometimes tossed off the covers at night, but he never complained when she pressed against him. His arms curved about her waist, pulling her close. Bare skin on bare skin. The warmth of breath. She fell asleep to his even breathing, the rise and fall of his chest.

And now he's gone, and there's nothing that can warm her. She has a weighted blanket. She piles her bed at home with pillows—heavy, body-length pillows on each side of her, enclosing her. Nothing helps. She has one of his old shirts. She holds it, presses it to her cheek, buries her face in it. She pretends that it still smells of him, even though she knows that the scent must be long gone.

She didn't bring his shirt to the lake house. She tells herself she doesn't need it, it doesn't smell of him. That in the house by the lake—the place he briefly loved—she'll be able to sleep without it.

She wakes from confused dreams, the blankets twisted around her. A memory of cold water, the beach at night. A lighthouse in the distance. She thinks she was calling someone's name. Shivering from cold. Sirens blaring on a highway above.

She walks into the kitchen and sees it: the blanket she tossed on the floor the night before, to soak up the puddle. It's still damp.

There was a girl here last night. It was real.

Numbly, Anna gathers up the blanket, tosses it in the laundry to wash later. She doesn't want to think of it. A girl wandering the woods and lakeshore, knocking on doors. Gone in an instant.

Anna makes coffee. Hot and black and strong. Mechanically, she scrambles eggs.

Only after does she remember the security camera. The one Brian set up last summer. Anna doesn't have the security app on her phone, so she has to log into the company's website to see the footage. She watches the porchlight turn on; she sees herself open the door. But she opens the door to no one.

Brian mentioned the ghost girl once. Anna remembers it now; an offhand remark— *They say not to drive too late on this road, not in the spring.* He was smiling. He didn't believe in ghosts, of course. It was just a bit of local trivia. He'd summered in the region as a kid with his family, heard some stories. A local urban legend: broken heart, car crash, death. He didn't mention it again. It never came up when they bought the house. Thinking back, Anna can't remember where on the highway they were when she heard the story. They drove up and down the coast on their summer vacations, exploring the little towns, beaches, lighthouses, parks. But in all their time together, they'd never come so early in the season. Now the beech trees are bare, the lake cold and gray. Businesses in the nearby town still closed, vacation homes empty.

There was a different emptiness in the city. The crowds streaming past her in the streets were filled with busy strangers, all walking briskly and engaged in their own purposeful lives. In her house, Brian's absence ballooned to fill every room. Anna had tired of it—she'd wanted to be alone and lonely in a different place. By the water, under open sky. Among bare trees and pines. To feel Brian's absence differently. His loss might have a softer presence here, she thought, spread throughout water and wood and sky. She found herself clenching the wheel hard as she drove out of the city, tension an ache in her jaw. Something loosened as the countryside opened up, as the miles stretched ahead. As the lake finally came into view. But when she opened the door to the silent, dark cottage, the grief hit her: a sneaker wave from a seemingly calm sea, knocking her off her feet, ripping away her breath, pouring in and through her in an endless flood.

He was only fifty-two.

She keeps thinking this, over and over. Even all these months later. When she first met him, they were in their twenties and she thought fifty-two ancient, an unfathomable age, the age of parents and professors and bosses. Old. And now fifty-two is young, far too young. Too *goddamn fucking young.*

'Jenny-of-the-Lake', she's called locally. She's been blamed for a string of purportedly mysterious deaths since the 1960s. A teen boy found frozen on the beach. Another who drove his car into a tree. A young man who never made his way home after a party, and was found dead in the woods. Perhaps the most disquieting cases are those of men found dead in their own homes. They either lived alone near the lake, or their families were away for the night. They were reportedly all in good health. And though there were no clear signs of foul play, they were found

stiff with cold even though they died in warm rooms.

My friends and I all knew these stories growing up. 'Don't open the door to Jenny!' we said. It was a game among us, to ring a friend's doorbell and then hide or run away. 'Don't open the door to Jenny!' we'd say as we ran.

—recollections of Jack Dykstra, age 66, from the article "Rural Ghost Stories of the Midwest", published on the website *Modern Folklore.*

Anna drives into town. For once, after the disturbance of last night, she doesn't want to be alone. She orders a meal at one of the few places open. There's a scattering of local customers at the Blue Mitten Grill: two men at the bar, a few occupied booths, a harried mother scolding her young children. Anna orders a sandwich and fries and eats without tasting a thing.

She lingers over a drink refill she doesn't need. Watches as a family of four walks in. As the waitress flirts with a customer. Have any of these people met the local ghost? What do they know?

"Anything else I can do for you, dear?" the waitress asks her.

Anna doesn't know how to bring up the ghost. She doesn't know how to talk to people—not anymore. She feels like a ghost herself, watching the living people in this restaurant as though through a thick pane of glass.

"No," Anna says. "I'm fine."

The knocking comes again that night. Anna's been waiting for it. Curled up on the couch, trying to watch TV, yet not registering anything at all. Even though she expects it, the first knock makes her jump. She clutches her blanket to her. Holds still as the hammering comes again and again.

The ghost eventually gives up, goes away. Anna stays where she is, and her heart keeps hammering long after ghost's knocks have faded.

She doesn't check the security footage this time. She doesn't want to see. Or not see.

Daylight lasts longer these days, but there are still traces of snow in the woods, little mounds and streaks of dirty-white, even as green shoots push up from the earth. Anna's still cold; that hasn't changed. She's turned up the thermostat, built up fires in the fireplace. Taken long, hot showers and baths. Wrapped herself in her bed comforter. She puts on every layer she has when she goes outside. The cold is in her bones. It doesn't leave.

'Lady in White' ghost stories have common themes of abandonment, betrayal, and loss. There is almost always a tragic love story involved. The ghost sometimes loses her lover to mishap or war, but more often he cruelly leaves her. She returns to the scene of her grief or death—pacing the widow's walk of a stately old manor, haunting the backstage of an abandoned theatre; materializing in the bathroom of the girls' school where she hung herself, or walking the stretch of lonely highway where her car ran off the road. She's usually a sad, passive presence: a vanishing face in a window, a hitchhiker

disappearing from the backseat when the driver turns around.

The story of Lake Jenny is an unusual example of the genre in that she isn't just a passively mourning spirit, a wistful figure in white. She takes on elements of a classic vengeance spirit: her grief is rage and desire with dire effects in the mortal realm. In her grief, she seeks and actively takes life from the living.

—from "Vengeance Spirits and Ladies in White: A Cross-Cultural Analysis of Female Ghosts" by Allison M. Lee in Journal of Global Folklore.

Anna spends most of the next day on the deck, staring out at the lake. Gray water under cold, gray skies. She lets the water, this vast inland sea, fill her sight. She lets her mind empty into the white-tipped waves, into the space where the water meets sky.

Her hands are numb when she finally stands, her whole body stiff.

She makes her way down to the beach. A flash of memory—bright sun, blue skies, and Brian turning over rocks at the shoreline, hunting for Petoskey stones, the state rock of Michigan. She can almost see him bent over in the water, the back of his neck reddening in the sun. She can almost touch him. They collected rocks together, piling them in little cairns on the beach, displaying them in glass containers. The glass containers are still here, sitting on shelves and on the kitchen table of the beach house. The little beach cairns are gone. She feels hot tears on her face. The wind is blowing. He's not here. He's not here, and all she wants is to hold him again, to see him, touch him, feel him. Talk to him. Tell him about the past few days, tell him everything, apologize yet again. Fling herself against him. She's cold. She's so cold, and she misses his warmth.

There's no knock on the door that night. The ghost has given up, Anna figures.

The ghost is knocking on other doors, haunting other houses. Walking the highway or beaches and dunes. Alone.

Over the next few days, the earth and air warm even if Anna doesn't. The sun breaks free. New green springs up from the forest floor, the understory leafing out beneath still-bare trees. The last traces of snow are gone, and birdsong fills the world. The sky is clear, and in its brilliant light Lake Michigan turns Caribbean blue.

The ghost is gone. Anna should be relieved. Instead, the hollowness in her chest only feels slightly bigger.

She spends an afternoon at the bookstore in town. Since Brian's death, she's had trouble reading for pleasure. Still, the presence of books is comforting—the shelves of stories around her, the heft of a book in her hands.

She finds what she was looking for. She takes it up to the counter.

"Ah," the owner says crisply as she rings up the 10th anniversary edition of *Haunted Tales and Legends of Lake Michigan's Shores*. "That's a classic. Has a few stories from right around here."

"Lake Jenny," Anna says, and she's surprised at how small, how childish, her own voice sounds.

"That's right." The store owner gives her a second look. She's a rather severe-looking older woman, gray hair pulled back in a bun. Anna doesn't think the other woman remembers her. She and Brian visited the store only a few times last summer. Last summer, the first season that they owned their first vacation home.

"Jenny is a sad story," the other woman says now, thoughtfully. Her demeanor has softened. "She's something of a boogeyman around here—something to scare kids with—but I always felt sorry for her."

Anna nods. "Me, too," she says.

Jenny doesn't return, but Anna can *feel* her out there in the darkness. Wet and freezing and desperate. Searching.

Looking for a lit window in the darkness. An occupied home on the empty lakeshore. Some sign of welcome or life. An open door. An outstretched hand.

Any offer of warmth.

Anna was especially cold last autumn.

Half-heartedly, she told Brian to stay away. To not kiss her. He didn't listen. She didn't expect him to.

She didn't *want* him to.

They never took particular care to avoid one another when sick. *I'll just get it, too*, Brian shrugged. Colds and flus—it wasn't really a big deal, was it? They still held each other. Slept in the same bed. Brian would grumble about the bunched-up tissues that she would leave scattered around the house, and clean them up. They would make each other soup.

This particular flu was the worst she'd had in years. A sudden headache, falling on her like a crushing stone. And then the bone-deep chills.

Her skin was hot to the touch, feverish. Her insides were ice.

She whimpered, snuggling into her husband's warmth. He held her from behind, spooning with her in bed, the heavy comforter piled on top. She couldn't get warm. He held her, he held her, one hand stroking her arm, her hair; she leaned back against him. In an aching, blurred landscape of pain and cold, he was the only warmth. She shivered and froze until she slept.

It *was* only the flu. The doctors verified this later.

They'd both had their flu vaccinations. They were both in good health.

Sometimes the vaccines aren't a great match for the circulating strains. A doctor friend once explained it to her: the science of how researchers try to predict which strains to immunize against each year.

Brian seemed to be getting better with his own bout of flu when his fever spiked. A deepening cough. Chest pain.

A bacterial secondary infection. Pneumonia, then sepsis. She should have gotten him to the doctor sooner. Insisted on it. A prescription of antibiotics would have stopped it, if they'd just gone in time. She should have urged him to get Tamiflu before the influenza—the first infection—could even take hold.

She should have stayed away from him. Not let him get sick in the first place. Locked herself in the guest room. Refused to let him touch her. Cuddle her, hold her.

It's okay, he said, holding her. *You know you're contagious before symptoms even show up, don't you? You've probably already given it to me.*

Survivor accounts of Jenny are generally reports of seeing her at a distance. A woman in white standing on the beach. A glimpse of her near the state park, on the highway, or in the parking lot of a motel. Contact isn't sustained; the witness doesn't see Jenny's eyes.

After the publication of the first edition of our book, we were contacted by many with personal stories of their own sightings of Jenny. An email from Ellen Rafferty of Chicago stood out, and we reached out to her for more. She claims that she was vacationing in the area with her family in 2019, staying in a rented home on the lake when Jenny knocked on her door.

"Rick and the kids had driven out to see a movie. It was one of those sci-fi action hero things, and I'm not really into that, you know? So I decided to stay in, have a quiet night to myself. It was around 10 when she knocked on the door. Scared the hell out of me.

"Of course I let her in. How could I not? I didn't know anything about ghosts. I just

saw this dripping wet girl, this kid, who needed help.

"She never said a word. Just looked at me with these big, dark eyes that seemed to see and not see me. Even as I was babbling my head off at her, saying, Oh my god, what happened? *and grabbing her a blanket. She was wearing a skimpy white dress, sleeveless. Too cold for the weather, even if she weren't also soaking wet. She was shaking, and her skin was so pale it was blue.

"She sat on the couch like I told her to, with my blanket wrapped around her. I said I would grab some dry clothes of mine for her to wear. But when I came back from the bedroom, she was gone.

"I still think of her. My family came home, and we called the cops to report a girl in need of help, but of course they never found her and there were no reports of anyone missing or hurt that night. Knowing what I do now, I'm glad I didn't touch her. I guess some part of me knew not to. But oh, she was lonely and cold. I could feel it. I really could. There was just. ... cold and desperation coming off of her. Like hunger. I wanted to comfort her. I didn't touch her, but I wanted to—to wrap that blanket around her myself, hug her in *it, towel her off, make sure she was dry and warm. Give her a cup of hot tea.*

"I know that she's dangerous. I even knew it that night. But I still feel for her. I wish she were okay."

— from Haunted Tales and Legends of Lake Michigan's Shores: Updated 10th Anniversary Edition. Storm Bay Press.

Jenny haunts the area for only a few weeks of early spring. That liminal time when flowers bloom and songbirds have returned, but winter's bite still lingers. She returns like an ephemeral wildflower of the woods—a brief vision of white, here and gone before most can even notice.

Anna puts down her copy of *Haunted Tales*. She counts off the days left.

She's felt Jenny's silent call every night. That screaming need. Her hammering on doors that don't open, on empty vacation rentals and homes that ignore her. Cars that drive past.

Anna's dreams now are always of blackness and cold water. It's almost a relief; at least she's sleeping again each night.

The cold that she feels—it isn't all her own.

She normally leaves the porch light off, letting it turn on only in response to motion. But tonight she deliberately switches the light on. It's a sign that someone's home. A welcome. A beacon.

She leaves all the lights on in her house.

When Jenny comes, Anna has the thick blanket ready. She doesn't need to take her eyes off the ghost.

"I'm sorry," she told her husband when he first caught her flu. When it was still just a flu.

"I'm sorry"—when he was shaking with chills, and she was the one holding him and keeping him warm.

"I'm sorry," the doctors said. "I'm sorry," people told her after he died. *I'm sorry, I'm sorry, I'm so sorry for your loss.*

Her throat was blocked. She couldn't speak.

She could hardly look Brian's family in the eye.

Afterwards, Brian's sister kept calling her, texting her, checking up on her. Asking if she wanted to get together for a coffee or lunch. Anna came up with excuses, or didn't answer at all.

Finally, she fled.

It's a rare complication, the doctor told her. There were so many doctors at the end, but this one seemed to be the main one, the one in charge. He said, *Many wrong things had to happen in just the wrong way. I'm sorry.*

Jenny steps in, and she's what Anna remembers: a thin white girl with long black hair down her back. Blue lips and huge eyes. Dripping with water.

Anna gets her wrapped up in the thick blanket, not touching her directly. She hands her a cup of hot tea.

Jenny sits on the couch, sipping. Her eyes staring over the rim of the cup, hungry and dark.

She puts down the cup. "I'm still cold," she says plaintively. Her voice is a little girl's. A lost little girl.

"I know," Anna says.

Why did she let Jenny in? Did she really think she could warm her, comfort her? Do what the woman in her book could not? Cold radiates from the ghost, the chilling atmosphere from an entire planet of winter.

Jenny stands up, clutching the blanket around her. She takes a step toward where Anna is standing. "I'm still cold," she repeats. And her eyes lock on Anna's, pleading. Anna doesn't move.

Is this how Jenny has ensnared boys and men over the years? Not just seducing with beauty—which the girl certainly has—but with an appeal to compassion, to human warmth? To the vanity of thinking you could save someone else?

She could be Anna's daughter. If she and Brian had had a daughter. She's the right age. She even has Anna's coloring: the dark hair and dark eyes.

"I'm sorry," Anna says, as the girl takes another step. Water drips to the floor, and Anna smells lake water.

It's not vengeance. Anna knows that in her bones. Jenny has never meant to take revenge, to hurt anyone. She's just seeking warmth, in the easiest way she can. Anna understands. She knows what it's like to contain a frozen sea within. To starve for human touch. To crave it so badly she thinks she'll go mad. To yearn for just a simple brush of fingertips, an exhalation of breath, a heartbeat near hers. To live off the memory of past warmth.

Jenny's eyebrows lift slightly. "You're cold like me," she tells Anna.

"Yes," Anna says.

Like and not like. Anna's body still holds its human warmth. But oh, she's cold, and her cold is nothing to Jenny's. Anna deserves to be cold—she *deserves* it—and Jenny's is far greater than Anna can carry on her own. Jenny's is an endless tundra of cold, a fathomless lake: vast, immeasurable. Jenny's cold can swallow Anna whole.

This is what Anna wants. This is why she turned on the porch light, why she opened the door. She'd thought she was just reaching out—that she didn't want to be alone. And she doesn't.

What she wants, she understands now, is to join Jenny's cold. To disappear in it. To merge into that endless tundra, melt into her dark lake. To join the other souls Jenny's swallowed—to lose herself among them. To no longer be herself. No longer alone with the cold, bearing it all on her own.

She reaches out for the shivering ghost girl. She steps into her eager embrace.

*See Vanessa Fogg's story "The Cold Inside"
online at Metaphorosis.
If you liked it, leave a comment. Authors love
that!
Remember to subscribe to our e-mail updates so
you'll know when new stories are posted.*

About the story

I'm fascinated by urban legends, our modern folklore. One such legend that shows up cross-culturally is that of the Woman in White, also sometimes known as the "White Lady". I think I was reading about her in late 2022. Around the same time, my family came down with a bad winter cold. It wasn't COVID (we tested), and we were all fine within a few days, but it was miserable at the time, as colds can be. COVID-19 was still very much in my mind, too, and I found myself thinking of the worst that could happen —of how it would be to feel responsible for someone you loved falling fatally ill. These things mixed in my mind and somehow created this story. Also, like Anna, I frequently feel cold when others don't.

A question for the author

Q: If your writing style were a bird, what type of bird would it be and why?

A: I like to think my writing would be a flock of starlings, individual words and sentences pretty but not overly showy, with subtle iridescence. And together, the starling-sentences would weave graceful patterns in the sky.

About the author

Vanessa Fogg dreams of selkies, dragons, and gritty cyberpunk futures from her home in western Michigan. She spent years as a research scientist in molecular cell biology and now works as a freelance medical writer. Her fiction has appeared in *Lightspeed, Podcastle, GigaNotoSaurus*, Neil Clarke's *The Best Science Fiction of the Year: Volume 4*, and more. She is fueled by green tea.

www.vanessafogg.com, @FoggWriter

A word about Candra Hope

Candra Hope is a marvelous artist whose characters are lived in, maybe weary — they've seen something of the world, and it hasn't always been happy. But I've been very happy with her work for *Metaphorosis*.

We were first in contact in mid-2016, but it took me until 2017 to commission a *Metaphorosis* cover from her. From then, she (also a member of Meta4osis) produced covers for the April and August 2017, May 2018 (a phenomenal image of an octopus), June 2018 (gryphons!), and August 2019 covers. The latter (with gauzy elephant, bear, and spider) is one of my favorite *Metaphorisis* covers ever.

I'm very happy to have her back providing the cover art for this issue, illustrating Vanessa Fog's "The Cold Inside". I urge you to look up her work!

About Candra Hope

My name is Candra Hope and I've been doing some sort of art since I was old enough to hold a pencil. I've always loved fantasy, horror and science fiction stories so thats mostly what inspires me, along with movies and nature and history and, well, whatever catches my soul at any given time. I work traditionally or digitally but refuse to use ai image generators because its non copyrightable and uses non consensually scraped art for training.

www.candrahopeart.com

Copyright

Title information

Metaphorosis Jan-Mar 2024

ISSN: 2573-136X (online)
ISBN: 978-1-64076-278-7 (e-book)
ISBN: 978-1-64076-279-4 (paperback)

Works of fiction

This book contains works of fiction. Characters, dialogue, places, organizations, incidents, and events portrayed in the works are fictional and are products of the author's imagination or used fictitiously. Any resemblance to actual persons, places, organizations, or events is coincidental.

All rights reserved

Moral rights asserted

Each author whose work is included in this book has asserted their moral rights, including the right to be identified as the author of their respective work(s).

Publisher

Metaphorosis Magazine is an imprint of
Metaphorosis Publishing
Neskowin, OR, USA

www.metaphorosis.com

"Metaphorosis" is a registered trademark.

Discounts available

Substantial discounts are available for educational institutions, including writing workshops. Discounts are also available for quantity purchases. For details, contact Metaphorosis at metaphorosis.com/about

Metaphorosis Publishing

Metaphorosis offers beautifully written science fiction and fantasy. Our imprints include:

Metaphorosis Magazine
Plant Based Press
Verdage
Vestige

You can also find us:
Metaphorosis@writing.exchange
@Metaphorosis
www.facebook.com/metaphorosis

Help keep Metaphorosis running by supporting us at
Patreon.com/metaphorosis

See more about some of our books on the following pages.

Metaphorosis Magazine

Metaphorosis

Metaphorosis is an online speculative fiction magazine dedicated to quality writing. We publish an original story every week, along with author bios, interviews, and notes on story origins.

We also publish monthly print and e-book issues, as well as yearly Best of and Complete anthologies.

Come and see us online at magazine.Metaphorosis.com.

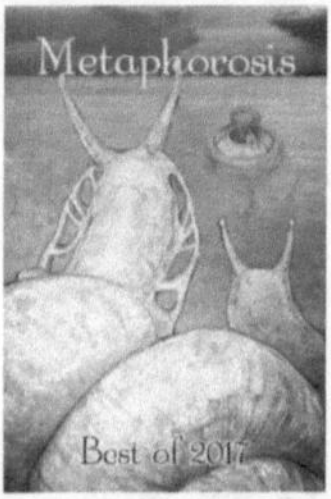

Plant Based Press

Vegan-friendly science fiction and fantasy, including anthologies of the year's best SFF stories, from 2016-2020.

Chambers of the Heart

speculative stories
by
B. Morris Allen

A heart that's a building, a dog that's a program, a woman sinking irretrievably — stories about love, loss, and motion.

Susurrus

A darkly romantic story of magic, love, and suffering.

Allenthology: Volume I

Including three full collections of SFF stories.

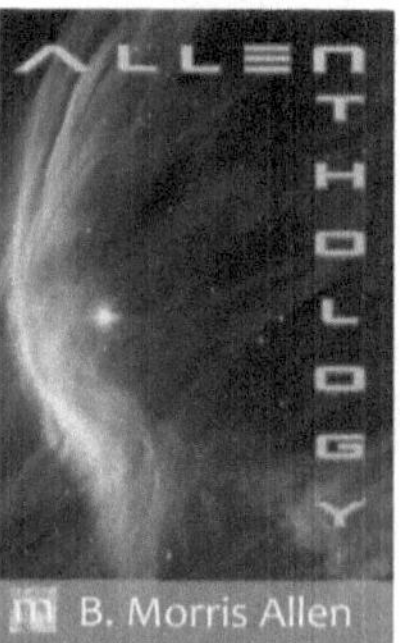

Verdage

Science fiction and fantasy books for writers — full of great stories, often with an additional focus on the craft of speculative fiction writing.

Reading 5X5 x3

Changes

How do stories move from 'maybe' to published?

Here are 15 case studies of stories published in *Metaphorosis* magazine.

Reading 5X5 x2

Duets

How do authors' voices change when they collaborate?

A round-robin of five talented science fiction and fantasy authors collaborating with each other and writing solo.

Including stories by Evan Marcroft, David Gallay, J. Tynan Burke, L'Erin Ogle, and Douglas Anstruther.

Score

an SFF symphony

An anthology with an emotional score from the heights of joy to the depths of despair – but always with a little hope shining through.

Reading 5X5

Five stories, five times

See how different writers take on the same material.

Reading 5X5

Writers' Edition

Two extra stories, the story seed, and authors' notes on writing.

Vestige

Novelettes, novellas, and novels by Metaphorosis authors.

The Nocturnals
Mariah Montoya

Night is Dangerous. Day is deadly.

Where day and night last thirty years, humans move constantly stay ahead of the night and cruel Nocturnals that call it home. But a boy is lost out there.

Joyful Heave

Science fiction and fantasy anthologies with innovative and unusual themes.

Museum Piece
an unusual collection

A gallery of the strange and outrageous

Step right up and enter a world of wonder and oddities! These museums are not your typical tourist traps. From the Museum of Lost Dreams to the Suicide Museum, each exhibit will take you on a journey you won't soon forget.

For the Unit always:
Mommy. Daddy. Nat Nat. Jeffy.
Ella. Roman. and Titan